Stink

Twice as Incredible

Megan McDonald

illustrated by Peter H. Reynolds

WALKER
BOOKS

First published as Stink: Twice as Incredible 2017 by Walker Books Ltd
87 Vauxhall Walk, London SE11 5HJ

4 6 8 10 9 7 5

This book has been typeset in Stone Informal

Printed and bound by CPI Group (UK) Ltd, Croydon CR0 4YY

British Library Cataloguing in Publication Data:
a catalogue record for this book is available from the British Library

ISBN 978-1-4063-7742-2

www.stinkmoody.com
www.walker.co.uk

MIX
Paper from
responsible sources
FSC
www.fsc.org   FSC® C020471

Stir

Megan McDonald

illustrated by

CONTENTS

SHORT,

SHORTER,

SHORTEST

Shrimp-o!

Runtsville!

Shorty Pants!

Stink was short. Short, shorter, shortest. Short as an inchworm. Short as a … stinkbug!

Stink was the shortest one in the Moody family (except for Mouse, the cat). The shortest second grader in Class 2D. Probably the shortest human being in the whole world, *including Alaska and Hawaii*. Stink was one whole head shorter than his sister, Judy Moody. Every morning he made Judy measure him. And every morning it was the same.

One metre, twelve centimetres tall. *Shrimpsville.*

He had not grown one inch. Not one centimetre. Not one hair.

He was always one head shorter than Judy. "I need another head," he told his mum and dad.

"What for?" asked Dad.

"I like your head just the way it is," said Mum.

"You need a new *brain*," said Judy.

"I have to get taller," said Stink. "How can I get taller?"

"Eat your peas," said Dad.

"Drink your milk," said Mum.

"Eat more seafood!" said Judy.

"Seafood?"

"Yes – *shrimp*!" Judy said.

"Hardee-har-har," said Stink. His sister thought she was so funny.

"What's so bad about being short?" asked Dad.

"I have to drink at the baby fountain," said Stink. "And stand in the front row for class pictures. And I always have to be a mouse in school plays. Just once, I'd like a speaking part, not a *squeaking* part."

"Being short isn't all bad," said Dad. "You still get those free colouring books you like at the doctor's."

"And the Spider-Man pyjamas you love still fit you," said Mum.

"And you still get to use your baby step stool just to brush your teeth," said Judy. Stink rolled his eyes.

"You'll grow," said Dad.

"Growing takes time," said Mum.

"Lie down on the floor," Judy told him.

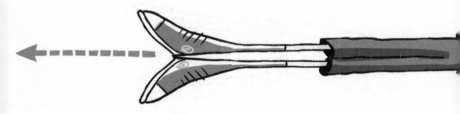

"What for?"

"If I pull your arms, and Mum and Dad each take a leg, we could stretch you out like a rubber band. Then you'd be taller."

Stink did not want to be a rubber band. So he ate all his peas at dinner. He did not hide even one in his nap-kin. He drank all his milk, and did not pour even one drop into Judy's glass when she wasn't looking.

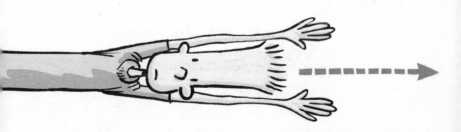

* * *

"Measure me again," Stink said to Judy. "One more time. Before bed."

"Stink, I just measured you this morning."

"That was before I ate all those peas and drank all that milk," said Stink.

Stink put on his shoes. He stood next to the Shrimp-O-Meter. He stood up straight. He stood up tall.

Judy got out her Elizabeth Blackwell Women of Science ruler. "Hey, no shoes!" she said. Stink took off his shoes. He stood on tiptoe.

"No tippy-toes either."

Judy measured Stink top to bottom. She measured him foot to head. She measured him head to foot. Something was not right.

"Well?" asked Stink.

"Bad news," said Judy.

"What?" asked Stink.

"You're shorter than you were this morning. Half a centimetre shorter!"

Stink made a face. "Not possible."

"Stink. The Women of Science ruler does not lie."

"Shorter? How can I be shorter?"

"Simple," said Judy. "You shrank!"

"You'll grow," said Dad.

"You'll grow," said Mum.

"But you'll never, ever, *ever* catch up with me!" said Judy.

The Adventures of Stink in Shrink Monster

BY STINK MOODY

The horrible Shrink Monster attacks the City of Moodyville!

ZAP!

EEEEK!

BEFORE

ZAP!

AFTER

Stink, the bravest (and shortest) kid in Moodyville, confronts the Shrink Monster!

GRRRRRR!

STOP!

ZAP

Huh?

Stink shrunk!

Max, fetch the Stink-Mobile.

Good boy, Max.

Will Stink have enough time to invent an un-shrinker? Or will Stink be attending Molecule Elementary School?

Stink-Mobile

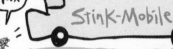

SHRINK, SHRANK, SHRUNK

When Stink woke up the next morning, his bed felt as big as a country. The ceiling was up there with the sky. And it was a long way down to the floor.

When he went to brush his teeth, even the sink seemed too tall.

"Yikes! I really am shrinking," said Stink, checking himself out in the mirror. Were his arms a little shorter? Was his head a little smaller?

Stink got dressed. He put on up-and-down-striped trousers and an up-and-down-striped shirt.

"What's with the stripes?" asked Judy.

"Makes me look taller," said Stink.

"If you say so," said Judy.

"What?"

"If you really want to look taller, here's what you do." Judy handed him a fancy shampoo-type bottle. "Put this hair gel on your hair and leave it in for ten minutes. Then you'll be able to comb your hair so it sticks straight up. Sticking-up hair will make you look taller."

Stink put the gooey gloop in his hair. He left it in his hair while he made his bed. He left it in his hair while he packed up his backpack. He left it in his hair all through breakfast.

"We could play baseball, and you could be *short*stop," Judy told him.

"So funny I forgot to laugh," said Stink.

Judy pointed to Stink's hair. "Hey, I think it's working!" she said.

"Really? Do you think people will notice?"

"They'll notice," said Judy.

Stink ran upstairs to look in the mirror. "HEY! My HAIR! It's ORANGE!"

"Don't worry," said Judy. "It'll wash out … in about a week."

"I look like a carrot!" said Stink.

"Carrots are tall," said Judy, and she laughed all the way to the bus stop.

✱ ✱ ✱

Stink's friend Elizabeth sat next to him in class. They were the shortest kids in Class 2D, so they sat at the front. "Hi, Elizabeth," said Stink.

"I'm not Elizabeth any more," she told Stink. "From now on, call me Sophie of the Elves."

"OK. I have a new name, too. The Incredible Shrinking Stink."

"But, Stink, you look taller today," said Elizabeth.

"It's just the hair," said Stink. "I'm still short."

"Not to an elf. To an elf, you'd be a giant. To an elf, you would be the Elf King."

"Thanks, Sophie of the Elves," said Stink.

The bell rang, and Mrs Dempster passed out spelling words. Three of the new words were *shrink, shrank, shrunk*. At lunch, the dessert was strawberry *short*cake. And in Reading, Mrs Dempster read everybody a book called *The Shrinking of Treehorn*.

The book was all about a boy who plays games and reads cereal boxes and gets shorter and shorter. He keeps shrinking and shrinking. Then, just when he becomes a normal size again, he turns green!

"Any comments?" Mrs Dempster asked when the story was over.

Stink raised his hand. "Is that a true story?"

Mrs D. laughed. "I'm afraid not," she said. "It's fantasy."

"Fantasy's my favourite!" said Sophie of the Elves. "Especially hobbits and elves."

"Are you sure it's fantasy?" asked Stink. "Because that kid is a lot like me. Because I'm ... I'm..." Stink could not make himself say *shrinking*.

"Because you both turned another colour?" asked Webster.

"Um, because I like to read everything on the cereal box, too," said Stink.

"OK," said Mrs Dempster. "Let's see. Who's going to carry the milk from the canteen today?" Stink was barely paying attention. He never got asked to carry the milk.

"How about Mr James Moody?" asked Mrs Dempster.

"Me?" asked Stink. He sat up taller. "I get to carry the milk?"

Stink walked down the second grade corridor. It looked longer than usual. And wider. He took the stairs down to the canteen. Were there always this many stairs? His legs felt shorter. Like they shrink, shrank, shrunk.

Stink got the milk crate. He carried the milk up the stairs, past the office, and past the staff room. Now his arms felt shorter. He needed a rest. He set the milk down outside the nurse's office.

"Hi, Stink!" called Mrs Bell. "I see you have a new hairstyle."

"My sister turned it ORANGE," said Stink.

"So, what brings you here today? Headache? Sore throat? There's a lot going around, you know."

"Is shrinking going around?" asked Stink. "Because I think I'm shrinking.

As in getting shorter."

"You're shrinking? What makes you think so?"

"My sister. I mean, she measures me every morning. And I'm always one metre, twelve centimetres. But last night she measured me before I went to bed, and I'd shrunk! I was only one metre, eleven and a half centimetres. I'm a whole half a centimetre shorter!"

"Don't worry, honey," said Mrs Bell. "Everybody shrinks during the day. We're all a little shorter at night than we are in the morning."

"Seriously?"

"Seriously. From gravity, and all the walking around we do, the pads between our bones shrink during the day. At night they soak up water and expand again."

"We all shrink?" asked Stink.

"That's what I'm saying. Everybody shrinks."

"Scientific!" said Stink.

The Adventures of Stink
in King of the Elves

BY STINK MOODY

Beautiful Sophie of the Elves falls under the dreaded gravity spell.

UP,
UP,
UP

Stink walked tall down the corridor, around the corner, and back to class 2D.

"Stink! You won!" said Sophie of the Elves.

"While you were gone," said Mrs Dempster, "we drew a name to see who would get to take Newton home this weekend. Your name was chosen."

"For real? Me? I get to take the newt home?"

"You have all the luck," said Webster.

"Things are definitely looking up, up, UP," said Stink, telling himself a joke and cracking himself up, up, up.

* * *

Stink climbed on the bus. He held the Critter Keeper carefully in his lap. "Don't worry, Newton," said Stink. "I'll take really good care of you. The best."

"What's that?" asked Judy when she got on the bus.

"A red-spotted newt. Like a baby salamander. His name's Newton."

"Where'd you get him?"

"He's our class pet. We're studying life-cycles, and Mrs D. went to New Hamster and brought him back for us. I'm taking care of him for the weekend. I get to play with him and watch him and keep a journal of stuff that happens."

Judy snorted. "New *Hampshire*, Stink. Not New Hamster."

"You mean *Newt* Hampshire!" said Judy's friend Rocky.

"It's in *Newt* England," said Judy, cracking up. Stink rolled his eyes.

* * *

When Stink got home, he did not stop to get a snack. Not even Fig *Newtons*. He took Newton up to his room. He got out his notebook and wrote:

Friday 3:37 Newton hiding

Stink stared at the newt. Judy came in and peered over his shoulder.

Friday 3:40 Newton hiding

Friday 3:45 Newton still hiding

"You should write BORING in your journal," said Judy.

"Newts are not boring," said Stink.

"Name one UN-boring thing about a newt," said Judy.

"Newts eat crickets. And worms and slugs," said Stink.

"BOR-ing!" said Judy.

"Red-spotted newts are the state amphibian of New Hampshire."

"BOR-ing," said Judy.

"OK. How about this? Newts start out as eggs. Then they hatch and swim around like tadpoles. Then they turn into red newts and live on land. Then they change colour and go back into the water."

"Now that's a teensy-weensy bit not-boring," said Judy.

"And they shed their skins," Stink said.

"Interesting!" said Judy. "Call me when *that* happens."

∗   ∗   ∗

On Saturday, Stink wrote in his journal some more.

10:52	Newton sniffed at worm
10:53	Newton sniffed at fake turtle
11:00	Newton ate cricket — whole!
11:30	Newton climbed up on new rock
11:36	Misted Newton with spray bottle
11:38	Newton stared at magazine picture of pond
11:45	Newton sleeping
12:00	Newton hiding
12:06	Still hiding

"Stink, are you going to stare at that newt all weekend?" asked Judy.

"I'm building him a raft. Out of Lego. Maybe he'll come out and float."

"You know what would be really UN-boring?" asked Judy. "Put the newt in with Toady."

"No way!" said Stink. "Newts are like poison to toads."

"So that means Toady won't eat him. C'mon, Stinker. Toady's all lonely." Before Stink could say Fig Newton, Judy scooped up Newton in her hands.

"You're supposed to wash your hands," said Stink. "Don't drop him."

"I won't drop him." She set him down on some moss in Toady's tank.

Newton sniffed at Toady and curled up his tail. "He's scared!" said Stink.

"Wait," said Judy. Toady licked Newton.

"Take him out!" yelled Stink.

"It was just a friendly lick," said Judy. "A newt lollipop."

"What if Toady gets poisoned? Get him out. Get him out!"

"Don't lay an egg!" Judy picked up Newton in her not-washed hand. "Stink! Something bad is happening to Newton. His head is splitting open."

"Let me see!" Stink peered at the

newt. Sure enough, Newton's skin had split, starting right at his head.

"He's shedding his skin!" said Stink. "Put him back! Put him back!"

They peered at Newton. "Do you think it'll really come off?" asked Stink.

"Sure," said Judy. "It means he's growing. Unlike *some* people."

"Even a newt grows more than me," said Stink.

"BOR-ing. I wish something would happen," said Judy. She leaned over and wrote in Stink's journal:

1:15 Boring!

Stink erased it. "Growing takes time," he told Judy. "That's what everybody always tells me."

"Maybe if we say some magic words," said Judy.

"Eye of newt,
Blah blah blah,
Wool of bat,
Tongue of toad."

"It's happening!" said Stink.

"Rare!" said Judy. She ran to get the video camera. "Lights! Camera! Action!" Stink took out his journal and wrote:

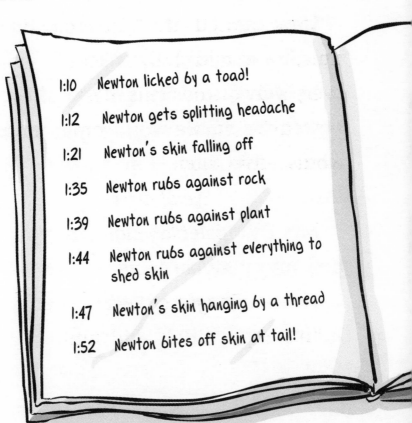

1:10	Newton licked by a toad!
1:12	Newton gets splitting headache
1:21	Newton's skin falling off
1:35	Newton rubs against rock
1:39	Newton rubs against plant
1:44	Newton rubs against everything to shed skin
1:47	Newton's skin hanging by a thread
1:52	Newton bites off skin at tail!

"Gross!" said Judy. She stopped the camera.

"Sweet!" said Stink, staring at the newt skin.

"Hey, can I have it?" asked Judy. "To show my class, I mean?"

"No way!" said Stink. "You already showed the whole world my dried-up baby bellybutton. I'm showing *my* class."

"Mrs Dumpster would want you to show my class, too."

"Not if you keep calling her Mrs Dumpster."

Stinkerbell, Shrinkerbell

P.U.! What's that smell?" Judy held her nose.

"What smell?"

"That dead-skunk smell. That one-hundred-year-old-dirty-sock smell. That three-hundred-year-old-rotten-egg smell." Judy walked around Stink's room, sniffing here, sniffing there. "It gets super-stinky as soon as you get close to Newton."

"Newton!" cried Stink. He sprang up from the floor, where he'd been drawing comics. Newton was in his hidey-hole. "Maybe it's the chopped-up dead worms in there. And dried-up crickets. Why isn't he eating?"

"Grody, grody, gross! There's green-y slime everywhere," Judy said.

"And brown stuff floating in the water."

"Stink, you have to clean it every day. Newts can die if their water gets too dirty."

"Since when are you the newt genius?"

"Since I read it in *Newtsweek*

magazine. You have to dump out the yucky water and wash the rocks and clean off all the slime and stuff."

"That's a lot of homework!" Stink said.

"C'mon, Stinkerbell. I'll help. We'll be the Slime Busters."

"Slime Busters! Double cool!" said Stink. "But you can't call me Stinkerbell."

"If you say so, Stinkerbell. Let's take it down to the big sink." Stink carried the Critter Keeper down to the kitchen, but he couldn't reach the sink.

"Here, let me," said Judy. She took the Critter Keeper from Stink and set it on the counter. Stink stood on a kitchen chair.

"First we have to get Newton out so we can clean his house. Stink, hold this jar. Let's put Newton in there."

"OK," said Stink, holding a tiny net. Judy reached in to scoop out Newton with her hand.

"The net!" cried Stink. "Mrs D. says use the net for scooping him out."

"Hold on. Wait. I almost have him. Ha, ha!" said Judy. "Gotcha, you little newt-brain!"

"He is not a newt-brain," said Stink. "And ... you're scaring him."

"He sure is slippery," said Judy. "You should call him Squirmy."

Just then, Squirmy squirmed right out of Judy's hand, slipped into the sink and went *SLOOP!* right down the drain.

"Newton!" cried Stink. "You LOST him!" he yelled at Judy.

"Don't worry, Stink," said Judy. "He's probably just swimming around down there under the sink." Judy peered down the drain.

"Is he there?" asked Stink. "Do you see him?"

"I can't see," said Judy. "It's dark… I need a flashlight or something. No. Wait. Let me turn the light on."

Judy flicked the switch over the sink. *GRRRRRRR!* A loud, grinding-up sound made them both jump back.

"STOP!" yelled Stink.

Judy turned off the switch. "Oops. Wrong switch."

"You killed Newton!" cried Stink. "The state amphibian of New Hampshire. My class pet. My homework!"

Stink ran to his room. He threw himself face down on the bed.

Newton was gone. Gone, *goner*, gon*est*. All that was left of Stink's class pet was his not-boring newt skin.

Stink gave the newt skin a place of honour on his desk. Right next to his gold Sacagawea dollar, his state quarters, and his French cootie catcher.

The newt skin just sat there. Lonely. Empty. Dead.

Deader than a doorknob.

Stink decided to do his homework. Homework always made him feel better.

Stink drew a still life of the newt skin for art class. He read a poem called "Who Has Seen the Wind?" He wrote one called "Who Has Seen the Newt?" and he used all his homework phrases in sentences.

Taking care of a newt is **easier said than done.**

*I hope Newton does not **get cold feet** out on the river.*

If your class pet goes down the drain, **go back to the drawing board.**

Judy came up to his room. "I'm sorry, Stink," she said. "I'm super-duper sorry. But I bet Newton slipped right down the pipes and on down to the river before I even flipped the switch."

Stink put down his pencil. "You think?"

"Newton is having the time of his

life. Think of it like *Stuart Little*. He's probably sailing down the river right now on a raft, having a big, fat, newt adventure."

"What am I going to tell Mrs Dempster? And my class?"

"They'll understand. It's all part of the life-cycle, Stink."

"The garbage disposal is NOT part of the life-cycle!" said Stink.

Stink finished his homework. He wrote the last entry in his journal.

Sunday 5:21 NEWTON GOES DOWN THE DRAIN

The Famous Jameses

On Monday morning, when Stink told Mrs D. about the GDI (Garbage Disposal Incident), she said, "Let's just tell the class Newton ran away. It'll be our little secret." She wasn't even angry. She told Stink she was going back to New Hampshire for Presidents' Day weekend, and she could get another newt.

Class 2D wrote stories about the adventures they thought Newton was having in the big, wide world. Webster wrote about Newton joining a baseball team called the Newt York Yankees. Sophie of the Elves wrote about a magic kingdom where Princess Salamandra was under an evil spell and a newt in shining armour came to rescue her. And Stink wrote about Newton sailing down the river on a raft to Legoland and riding the roller coaster.

The stories made everybody feel much better. Especially Stink. Mrs D.

even told Stink he could keep Newton's skin. As in, for real. For good. For *ever*.

∗   ∗   ∗

Mrs Dempster talked about Presidents' Day for the rest of the week. Stink's class made cotton-wool-ball portraits of George Washington. They made milk-carton-and-pretzel-stick log cabins in honour of Abraham Lincoln. Everybody said how tall Abe was. How tall his hat was. Tall, tall, tall. They acted like Abraham Lincoln was a giant.

"What's so great about living in a log cabin?" Stink asked Webster.

"Lincoln carved his maths problems on the walls, right in the logs."

"He should have got in trouble for writing on the walls!" Stink said.

All week, nobody said a word about Stink's favourite president, James Madison. Not one peep. James Madison had a birthday, too. March 16.

Mrs Dempster told the class, "OK, 2D. Homework is on the board."

What does Presidents' Day mean to you?

"I know! I know!" said Calvin.

"Presidents' Day means you see flags."

"It means we don't have school on Monday," said Webster.

"It means you can buy stuff on sale, because presidents are on money," said Heather S.

"Let's not give away all our ideas," said Mrs D. "I want everybody to write one page about what Presidents' Day means to *you*."

"Can we draw something, too?" asked Lucy.

"Can we write a poem?" asked Sophie of the Elves.

"Can we dress up?" asked Stink.

"Yes, yes, and yes," his teacher said. "But I still want my one page."

Stink took out his Big Head book of presidents. He flipped to the best president ever. President number four, James Madison.

Stink and James Madison were very alike. James Madison was from Virginia. Stink was from Virginia. James Madison had the name James. Stink had the name James! James Madison wore trousers. Stink wore trousers! Same-same!

More people should know about James Madison. They should have a statue of James Madison in the park. Or carve his head on the side of Mt Trashmore. They should sing about him in the state song.

That gave Stink an idea. A great big Presidents' Day idea.

* * *

All the way home from school, Stink made up words for the state song. He sang it to the tune of *Frère Jacques*. He sang it for Mum. He sang it for Dad.

"*Ja-ames Mad-i-son*
Ja-ames Mad-i-son
Num-ber four, num-ber four
Changed his hair to white
Wrote the Bill of Rights
Ding, dang, dong
We love you."

"That's great!" said Mum. "I don't think we have a Virginia state song."

"There's a state bird. And a state flower," said Dad.

"And a Virginia state quarter," said Judy.

State quarter! Of course! Lincoln was on a penny. Washington was on a dollar. James Madison should be on the Virginia state quarter!

"Can I use your smelly markers?" Stink asked Judy.

"No," said Judy. "You never put the caps back on."

"Newton," said Stink. "N-E-W-T-O-N.

Poor little newt. *GRRRRRRR.*" Stink made a garbage disposal noise.

"Oh, go ahead," said Judy. "But that's IT. I'm not going to let you keep pulling a NEWTON on me!"

Stink sniffed a grape marker. He sniffed a blueberry marker. He sniffed a black liquorice marker. *Yum, yum!*

He drew an outline of James Madison's head. On either side of it, he drew a quill pen and a number 4. Below it he wrote *E Pluribus Constitution.*

Then he wrote a letter to the governor.

Dear Mr Governor,

You should make a James Madison Virginia state quarter. James Madison is way better than ships. Please tell me when you make the new quarter.

I am in second grade at Virginia Dare School. I have a bossy big sister and a cat named Mouse and I had a newt that reached the end of his life-cycle.

Signed,

James E. Moody

P.S. Did you know you are governor of a state with no song?

The Adventures of Stink
in Newt in Shining Armour

By Stink Moody

Princess Salamandra is chased by the Evil Fly Dragon

I'm hungry!

MAGIC SPELL POPPY FIELD

... into the enchanted poppy field.

The Princess falls into a deep sleep.

Now I've got you, Princess!

ZZZZZZ

NOT SO FAST!

It's Newt in shining armour! He has FLY Dragon's favourite food – Liquorice!

YUM!

See you later, FLY Dragon!

Tumble, Fluff, Shrink!

Mum! Stink's doing homework again!" Judy said.

"You can't tell on me for doing homework," said Stink.

"Homework, schmome-work. Let's do something good."

"My homework's good."

"What's your homework?" asked Mum.

"Presidents' Day."

"You're not dressing up as a human flag again, are you?" asked Judy.

"No. I have to tell what Presidents' Day means to me."

"Stink, everybody knows what Presidents' Day means. Presidents' Day means your teacher reads you a book about George Washington's teeth and Abraham Lincoln's beard. Presidents' Day means you make stuff out of lollipop sticks, like a log cabin or a flag."

"Nuh-uh," said Stink.

"Presidents' Day means you draw three circles. One for Lincoln, one for Washington, and one in the middle for the stuff that's the same about both."

"It's called a Venn diagram," Mum said.

"My homework is what it means to *me*. Not what it means to Mr Venn."

"Good for you," Mum said. "What *does* Presidents' Day mean to *you*?"

"Two words," said Stink.

"Washington and Lincoln," said Judy.

"James Madison," said Stink.

Stink got out a bag of cotton wool balls. Stink made an old-timey James Madison wig. Judy helped him glue cotton wool balls to her old Brownie cap.

"Pass the glue," said Stink. "Quit hogging."

"Not so much!" said Judy. Stink didn't listen. He just kept gluing more cotton wool balls. "Let's see how it looks," said Stink.

"It has to dry first, or all the cotton wool balls will fall off," Judy told him.

"Let's dry it in the tumble dryer, then," Stink said.

"Genius!" said Judy.

Stink put the wig in the dryer. "Press START," said Stink. "I can't reach."

Judy pressed the fluff-and-tumble button. They waited. *Ga-lump, ga-lump.* They waited some more. The buzzer went off. *"Voilà!"* said Judy, pulling out the wig.

"YIKES!" yelled Stink. "I said press START. Not SHRINK. Now it looks like … an elf wig. An *ant* wig."

"YOU put it in the dryer," said Judy.

"YOU pressed the button," said Stink.

"Never mind. We can put powder in your hair. Like James Madison."

"You mean *I* can put powder in my

hair," said Stink. "Just to make sure it doesn't turn orange or anything."

"BOR-ing," said Judy.

✳ ✳ ✳

On Friday, Webster read his report aloud first. It was about making red, white and blue potholders at his grandpa's nursing home on Presidents' Day.

"Presidents' Day means to me that we should have a girl president," said Sophie of the Elves. "Since we don't, I wrote a poem about a First Lady. Stink told me about her, and I found out more. Her name is Dolley Madison."

Dolley Madison, first to be called First Lady.

On a fifteen-cent stamp.

Liked to dance and fish and cook and ride horses.

Looked like a queen.

Easter egg hunt, started it.

Yum! Cupcakes are named after her.

Married James Madison.

Always won running races.

Died in 1849.

Ice cream always dessert at the White House.

Saved a painting of George Washington from a fire.

Ostrich feathers in her hats.

Nice lady!

Last of all was Stink. He wore black.
He pinned a number 4 to his shirt. He
put white powder all over his hair.

WHAT PRESIDENTS' DAY
MEANS TO ME

by James Moody

*James Madison was the shortest president
ever. He was only one metre, sixty-two
centimetres tall, but he did great things.*

*Presidents' Day means we should not
forget about the shortest president ever,
James Madison. Everybody knows the
tallest. But nobody knows the shortest. He
was called "little Apple-John". They said
he was "no bigger than a half piece of
soap". That's a quote.*

*If you want to be president, it's good
if your name is James. There are a lot of
famous Jameses.*

"Hey! Your real name is James, too," said Webster.

"Exactly." Stink grinned. He finished reading his report.

Six presidents had the name James, so it must be lucky. James Madison had the name James. He was clever. He wrote the Bill of Rights. He was Father of the Constitution.

James Madison had eight brothers and sisters. If you're president, you get to boss even your big sister. He wore black. He put white powder in his hair to look older. He liked ice cream. He had a pet parrot. No lie. He loved science stuff, like the insides of rabbits. If James Madison was alive, he'd be over 250 years old.

My report is short because James Madison was short, too.

James Madison should be a quarter. James Madison should be a day off.

The End

The Adventures of Stink
in The Return of the Shrink Monster BY STINK MOODY

The Shrink Monster is back and he's MAD!

GRRRR!!

GULP!

What a headache!

He's about to throw Stink into the supersonic tumble dryer to shrink him to nothing!

But Stink pushes the Monster into the dryer instead!

Stink pushes the button...

ON

He watches the monster SHRINK...

into a ball of lint!

President James Madison presents Stink with a medal and reward money!

$

yay, stink!

Tall,
Taller,
Tallest

It was Not-James-Madison-Day on Monday. No school. Judy poked her head into Stink's room. "Stink, I'm supposed to be nice to you."

"Did Mum say?"

"Yep."

"Because of the newt?"

"Yep. And I'm supposed to make you feel taller or something. So, Stinkerbell, how about a birthday party?"

"A birthday party? For who?"

"Come downstairs and see."

Stink raced down the steps, two at a time.

Mum brought out twenty cupcakes on a big plate. They each had a letter on them, and all together, they spelled HAPPY JAMES MADISON DAY.

Dad lit the candles.

Everybody sang the James Madison State Song. Stink blew out all twenty candles. He ate an *M*, an *A*, and half of a *D*. Two and a half cupcakes!

"Presents!" said Judy.

"Presents? It's not even anybody's real birthday," said Stink.

"It's James Madison's un-birthday," said Judy.

"Dad and I made you a card," said Mum. "A Presidents' Day card."

"It was kind of short notice," said Dad. "So we printed some stuff off the Internet." Stink opened the card. It had pictures of short people.

At the bottom of the card, Mum and Dad had printed in big letters:

YOU'RE ONLY AS SHORT AS YOU FEEL!

"I found the famous Wrestler Guy," said Judy.

"Thanks!" said Stink.

"Now mine," Judy said. Stink ripped it open. "It's a fun mirror!" Judy told him. "From Rocky's old magic kit. I made it into a presidents mirror. One side is the James Madison side and the other is the Abraham Lincoln side."

Stink looked at himself in the James Madison side of the mirror. He looked super-shrimpy, and wide as a warthog. Everybody cracked up.

"Try the other side!" said Judy. Now

Stink looked as skinny as a pencil and as tall as Abe Lincoln.

"UN-Presidents' Day is better than Presidents' Day any time," said Stink. "WOW backward!"

"W-O-W backward is *wow*, too," said Judy.

"Exactly," said Stink.

"Thanks, you guys," said Stink. "For the cupcakes and presents and stuff."

"The James Madison party was Judy's idea," said Dad.

"Yeah. Are you feeling any taller yet?" Judy asked.

"Maybe a little. Especially when I look in the Abe Lincoln mirror!"

"You know, you weren't always short," said Dad.

"Really?" asked Stink.

"Really?" asked Judy.

"You weren't short when you were a baby," said Mum. "You were long. Fifty-five centimetres long."

"What about me?" asked Judy.

"You were only about forty-eight centimetres," said Dad.

"HA!" said Stink. "You mean *I* was taller than *Judy* when I was born?"

"I guess you could say that," said Mum.

"HA, HA!" Stink elbowed Judy. "Shorty Pants!"

"ROAR!" said Judy.

"More cupcakes, anyone?" Mum asked. "Oops. Almost forgot. An envelope came for you, Stink. Special delivery. Looks like it's from the governor." Mum handed Stink the envelope.

"Open it! Read it out loud!" said Judy.

Stink read the letter.

Dear Mr James Moody,

Thank you kindly for your thoughts concerning the James Madison state quarter. Unfortunately, Virginia has already completed its state quarter programme. We have no plans to issue another one at present. However, we do appreciate your enthusiasm for our forefather James Madison. Did you know that James Madison has been featured on a US half dollar and also on a five-thousand-dollar bill?

Enclosed please find the James Madison Bronze Peace and Friendship Medal in honour of your interest in our fourth president.

Your Governor,
Jean MacDonald

"A five-thousand-dollar bill!" said Stink. "Double, triple, quadruple cool!"

The medal was a copper-coloured coin in a plastic case. On one side it said *James Madison, President of the United States, 1809*. On the other, it had a picture of two hands shaking in friendship.

Stink passed around his brand-spanking-new James Madison friendship coin for everybody to see. While his family "oohed" and "aahed", Stink picked up the presidents mirror. He turned it to the tall side and looked at his reflection.

Everybody says growing takes time, thought Stink. *It's all part of the life-cycle. One day, it's going to happen to me. Me! Mr James Moody!*

Stin

Megan McDonald   illustrated by

K

and the
Incredible
Super-Galactic
Jawbreaker

Peter H. Reynolds

for Joseph, Jodi and Matthew

M. M.

To Gary Goldberger, my super-galactic
creative partner on the journey

P. H. R.

CONTENTS

Kid in a Candy Shop

Gigantic!

Super-colossal!

Inter-galactic!

Stink stood smack in the middle of the Whistle Stop Sweet Shop. Shelves all around him were chock-full of sourballs, penny sweets (that cost ten cents), strawberry shoelaces, gummy money, fizzy dummies, spooky-eye gumballs, wax fangs, buttered-popcorn jellybeans, milk bottles, chocolate Scottie dogs and mood lollipops.

Then he saw it. Right smack in the middle of it all.

Hello! Welcome to Planet Jawbreaker!

Super-galactic jawbreakers! Stink reached to pick one up. It was an earth, a globe, a world unto itself. A speckled, sparkling planet. Bigger than a marble. Bigger than a rubber ball. Bigger than a golf ball. World's largest gobstopper! Or at least the biggest Stink had ever seen in his whole entire seven years on the planet.

Stink's sister, Judy, ran up to him. "Look, Stink, they have candy fried eggs and lollipops that play music and

real-and-true rainforest gum and best of all … gummy brains! I can't decide WHAT you're getting me!"

"Your brains are gummy if you think I'm buying you stuff," Stink told his big sister. Sometimes big sisters were so double-triple-quadruple bossy.

"C'mon, Stink. Don't be a sourball. You have a big fat five-dollar gift certificate."

"I earned it! Dad took me to the college, and I was in a study for short people. I had to answer really hard questions."

"Stink, I can't help it if I'm not short!

Please, pretty please, with gummy brains on top? Just one chocolate mobile phone? A candy shrimp? A diamond-ring lollipop? I know, I know! If you won't buy me sweets, how about this How-to-Make-Your-Own-Gum kit?"

"No, no, no, no and nope."

"C'mon, Stinker. Just one teeny-weeny sweet? How much can one penny sweet cost?"

"Ten cents. Some penny sweets cost twenty-five cents."

"Huh? How can something that costs a penny cost twenty-five cents?"

"Beats me," said Stink.

123

Stink's sister, Judy, was in a mood. She slumped down on the car-seat couch in the corner of the sweet shop. She pretended to watch the Oompa-Loompas dancing on the TV screen in front of her. Stink popped from one shelf to the next, filling his basket with suckers and sourballs, gumballs and jelly worms.

"Stink, I'm telling Dad you're acting like a kid in a candy shop," said Judy.

"But I AM a kid in a candy shop," said Stink. "Hey! You just said an idiom."

"I am NOT an idiot!" said Judy.

"Id-i-om. It's what you call a funny

saying. Mrs D. taught us a bunch of them. Like if you're in a bad mood, I could say you got out of the wrong side of bed."

"But I'm not in a bad mood, because you're going to get me some sweets, right?"

"Wrong."

"Is *stinks on ice* an idiom? How about *rotten to the core*?" said moody Judy.

"Now you're acting like sour grapes," said Stink. "Get it? *Sour grapes* is another idiom."

"Stop saying *idiom*!" said Judy.

"OK! OK! If I get you some sweets,

what will you give me?" asked Stink. "*Let's strike a deal.* Get it?"

Judy rolled her eyes. "How about one Grouchy pencil and two president baseball cards for this box of rainforest gum?"

"*Three* president baseball cards," said Stink. "And one of them has to be James Madison."

"Deal," said Judy. "Goody goody gumdrops! Thanks, Stink. Now, Richie Rich, let me see what you're getting yourself with all that money."

"I," said Stink, "am getting the World's Biggest Jawbreaker." He held it

up for Judy to see. "It changes colours and flavours as you go."

"Rare! It looks like an earth. Or a giant emu egg or something."

"Or something," said Stink.

"Stink, I don't think you want to

eat that. Says here on the box that it contains wax."

"Does not."

"Does too!" Judy pointed to the words on the box.

"So? I've eaten wax before."

"Have not."

"Have too."

"Stink, wax is like candles," said Judy. "Wax is like earwax. Are you going to eat EARwax, Stink?"

"Give it," said Stink, taking it back. "Stop saying *earwax*! I'm still eating it. It has fire in the middle."

"Like a fireball?"

"Like the earth's core!" said Stink.

"RARE!" said Judy. "Do you think it'll really break your jaw?"

"It'd better!" said Stink.

Finger-Lickin' Good

Stink took one lick. Then another. Then another. The giant jawbreaker was far too big to fit in his mouth.

Slurp. He licked that jawbreaker all the way home.

Sloop. He licked it all the way up to his room.

Slop. He licked it while he fed Toady one-handed. He licked it while he played with his president baseball cards (including James Madison, thanks to Judy). He licked it while he did his

homework one-handed. He licked it the whole time he talked to Grandma Lou on the phone, telling her all about the Pyjama Day they were going to have in Mrs D.'s class.

He even licked it while he set the table for dinner. One-handed, of course.

Pretty soon his lips were green and his tongue was blue and his hands were as sticky as gum on a shoe.

"Hey," Judy asked at dinner. "Why is there a big fat sticky blue fingerprint on my plate?"

"Oops," said Stink, licking his fingers. "Finger-lickin' good!"

"Stink's eating a jawbreaker for dinner!" said Judy, pointing.

"Stink, put that jawbreaker down and eat some real food," said Dad. "Here. Have some macaroni."

"This *is* real food," said Stink. "It contains vitamins A and C and calcium. No lie."

"And dextrose, sucrose, fructose and other stuff that makes you comatose," said Judy.

"It's NOT going to make me comb my toes," said Stink.

"And don't forget wax," said Judy.

"Macaroni," said Mum. "You heard Dad. And green beans."

"But it hasn't broken my jaw yet," said Stink. "It hasn't even stretched my mouth one bit."

"You already have a big mouth," said Judy.

"Hardee-har-har," said Stink. "Well, it hasn't set my tongue on fire yet or made my cheeks feel like a chipmunk, either."

"It may not break your jaw," said Judy, "but all your teeth are going to fall out. For sure and absolute positive. Did you know Queen Elizabeth I ate so many sweets from her pockets that her teeth turned black? No lie!"

"At least I won't have to brush them every day!" said Stink.

* * *

Every day, Stink ate a little more and a little more of his jawbreaker. He ate it in bed first thing in the morning, before he brushed his teeth. He ate it at playtime in between playing H-O-R-S-E with his super-duper best friend, Webster. He ate it on the bus and all the way home from school.

He gave a lick to Mouse the cat. He gave a lick to Toady the toad. He even tried giving a lick to Jaws the Venus flytrap.

Stink's jawbreaker went from super-galactic to just plain galactic. From golf-ball size to rubber-ball size.

"Are you still eating that thing?" asked Judy. Stink stuck out his tongue.

"Well, you look like a skink," said Judy. She pointed to his blue tongue.

Shloop! went Stink.

Stink ate his not-super-galactic jawbreaker for one whole week. He ate it when it tasted like chalk. He ate it when it tasted like grapefruit. He ate it through the fiery core to the sweet, sugary centre. He ate it down to a marble. A teeny-tiny pea.

Then, in one single bite, one not-jaw-breaking crunch, it was G-O-N-E, gone.

Stink was down in the dumps. He moped around the house for one whole day and a night. He stomped up the stairs. He stomped down. He drew comics. *Ka-POW*! He did not play with Toady once. He did not do his homework. He went outside and bounced Judy's basketball 117 times.

"Somebody got out of the WRONG side of bed," said Judy. "If I didn't know better, I'd think you were in a MOOD."

"I can have moods too, you know." Stink kept counting. "One hundred

and eighteen, one hundred and nineteen…"

"Is it because your jawbreaker's all gone?" asked Judy.

"It's because that jawbreaker lied. They should call it World's Biggest UN-jawbreaker. I ate and ate that thing for one whole week, and it did not break my jaw. Not once. It didn't even make

my mouth one teeny-weeny bit bigger.
See?" Stink clicked and clacked his
teeth open and shut.

"Maybe that's a good thing," said
Judy. "I mean, if it did break your jaw
for real, wouldn't you be mad?"

"Yeah, but instead I'm madder."
Stink had an idea. A brilliant
what-to-do-when-you're-mad
idea. Stink would write a letter.
A real-and-true official snail-mail letter.
A letter with a greeting and a body and
a closing, just the way Mrs D. taught
them in their how-to-write-a-letter unit
at school.

FROM THE DESK OF STINK MOODY

Dear Mr or Mrs Jawbreaker,

(THIS IS CALLED A GREETING)

My name is Stink Moody. I got $5 for being short and I spent it on a super-galactic jawbreaker (and some NOT-penny sweets for my sister).

There is a big problem with your jawbreaker. It did NOT (I repeat NOT) break my jaw. For your information, all it did was get me in trouble at the dinner table and make me look like a skink. In my opinion, you should change the name jawbreaker to Super Not-Galactic Mouth Crayon.

Yours Truly, ← (THIS IS CALLED A CLOSING)

Stink (THE SKINK) Moody

P.S. It did not even break the jaw of Jaws, my sister's Venus flytrap.

(THIS IS CALLED A POSTSCRIPT)

IDIOM COMICS presents

He Got Out of the Wrong Side of Bed

by Stink J. Moody

DONE! I JUST KNOW JUDY WILL LOVE THESE HAND-PAINTED EGGS.

HAPPY BIRTHDAY JUDY! YOU'RE A GOOD EGG!

I'LL HIDE THEM OVER HERE ON THE OTHER SIDE OF MY BED.

STINK WOKE UP THE NEXT DAY...

JUDY'S BIRTHDAY IS TODAY!

STINK JUMPED OUT OF BED...

AND LANDED RIGHT ON THE EGGS.

SMOOSH!!

WHY IS STINK SO GRUMPY?

HE MUST HAVE GOT OUT OF THE WRONG SIDE OF BED!

EGGS-ACTLY!

A Leopard Can't Change Its Spots

Exactly eleven days later, a parcel arrived for Stink. A box that thumped and clunked when he shook it. A box that rattled and crunched when he opened it. A big box full of ... jawbreakers!

Stink read the letter. "Dear Mr Stink Moody, blah blah. While we are not in the business of breaking jaws ... blah blah blah ... sorry that our jawbreaker did not meet your satisfaction ... more blah ... please accept an assortment of fun, exciting and brand-new jaw-breakers you might like…"

"Holy jawbreaker heaven!" There were mega jawbreakers, mini jawbreakers, monster jawbreakers, black, rainbow and psychedelic jawbreakers, asteroids and alien heads, glow-in-the-darks and gobstoppers, even jawbreaker lollipops on a stick with a bubblegum centre.

"Leaping lollipops!" squealed Judy. "Where'd you get all these? There's more jawbreakers here than in Willy Wonka's house." She tossed a handful up in the air.

"Five whole kilos!" said Stink. "It says so right here. Wait till I tell Webster!"

"That's 21,280 jawbreakers!" Judy pointed to the number on the box.

"What am I gonna do with twenty thousand million jawbreakers?"

"Get twenty thousand million cavities, of course," said Judy. "C'mon, let's divide them up. We can each set up our own jawbreaker shop and trade them with each other. Or we could start our own jawbreaker museum."

"What do you mean WE?" asked Stink.

"You and me," Judy said. "Two heads are better than one. I mean two *jawbreaker eaters* are better than one."

"No way are you getting half!" said Stink. "They're mine-all-mine, and I get to decide."

"Stink, you never share!"

"You know what they say … you can't teach an old dog new tricks! A leopard can't change its spots! Besides, I'm the one who wrote the letter."

"What letter?"

"I wrote a letter to the jawbreaker company about how my super-galactic jawbreaker did not break my jaw."

"No fair!" said Judy. "I wrote a letter once that you, my little brother, wrecked my Hedda-Get-Betta doll, and all I got from the doll company was a get-well card."

Stink cracked up.

"Are you sure you didn't win a contest for being short or something?" Judy asked.

"Honest! All I did was write one puny little letter."

 Suddenly, Stink had an idea. Not a puny little idea. A great big super-galactic idea.

If Stink could write one letter, he could write two ... three ... four!

It would be just like homework. Mrs D. said practice makes perfect. If he wrote more letters, he could get more free stuff. And if he got more free stuff, he'd be like a bazillionaire!

Stink took out his best writing-a-real-letter paper. At the top it said, FROM THE DESK OF STINK MOODY.

Stink started to write. He wrote and wrote and wrote. He used his best-ever A+ handwriting. He wrote until his hand felt like it was falling off. Three whole letters! Mrs D. would give him a triple Golden Pen rubber stamp for extra, extra, extra credit.

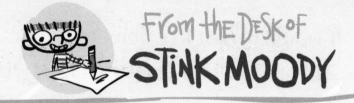

FROM THE DESK OF
STINK MOODY

Dear Kandy Kompany,

Did you know your Kool Katz chocolate bar is spelled wrong? Everybody, even the World's Worst Speller, my sister Judy, knows CATS is spelled C-A-T-S. Not K-A-T-Z. I think the name of your company is spelled wrong, too. Maybe you never heard of the letter C? (Comes after A and B!) In your ads, you say "Gimme a break!" I say, "Give ME a break."

Signed,

Stink

P.S. Your chocolate is funny too. It's WHITE!

FROM THE DESK OF
STINK MOODY

Dear Robo Toys,

I got a microbot with my lunch at House of Burgers. At first, it was way cool. It has eyes that light up and ears that go up and down, and it is called Burp, but I guess you know that. You say on your package that your mini robots will listen and do what I tell them. You say they will amaze me. I told Burp to mess up my sister's room. He did not mess up one thing! All he did was burp at the dinner table. It amazed me that I didn't get in trouble.

I even read all the directions. I mean ALL. Even the French ones.

Sincerely Un-amazed,

Stink

P.S. It says an astronaut thought up my toy. Maybe you should send the Amazingly Boring Burp back to outer space.

FROM THE DESK OF
STINK MOODY

Dear City Parks,

I went to a park near my house called Monkey Island. First of all, can I just tell you it is not an island. Second of all, there are NO monkeys. I looked up in the trees, in the jungle gym, behind rocks. I even looked in the bins. P.U.! I did not see one single monkey the whole entire time. Not even a monkey bar! My sister knows big dictionary words, and she said this is called false advertising. I could really do with some tickets to the zoo to see some real monkeys. And lemurs.

In closing,

Stink

It Never Rains, But It Pours

Once he started, Stink could not stop writing letters. He wrote a letter to Webster (the friend, not the dictionary). He wrote a letter to his other best friend, Elizabeth, who liked to be called Sophie of the Elves. He even wrote a letter to his teacher, telling her how great he was at writing letters.

At school, when Mrs Dempster put a sample letter on the board, full of mistakes, Stink found every single one, including *Deer Sirs* and *Yours Untruly*.

"Stink, you really put your thinking cap on today!" said Mrs D. "Now, who can tell me what the best part of writing a letter is?" she asked.

"When you've finished?" asked Webster.

"Cool stamps?" asked Sophie of the Elves.

"When somebody writes back!" said Mrs D.

"Especially when they write back

Aa Cc Dd Ee Ff Gg Hh Ii Jj Kk Ll Mm Nn Oo Pp Qq Rr Ss

ear
er Sirs,   writing
e are righting to ask ewe
r information about you're
ocolate company.
ours Untruly,
oom 2D

TODAY'S LESSON
Writing letters

with like about a million jawbreakers," said Stink.

"Speaking of a million, it's time for maths," said Mrs D.

✳ ✳ ✳

Waiting sure was bor-ing. UN-amazing. Stink came home from school and checked the post first thing every day. He did not get one puny letter. Not even a postcard! Not from the company that couldn't spell *cat*. Not from the toy company with the microbot that wouldn't listen. Not from the city park with no monkeys. Nothing. Nada. Zip. Zero.

"Maybe my letters got lost," said Stink.

"Maybe they know you're just trying to get free stuff," said Judy.

"Am not."

"Are too."

"Maybe I forgot to put stamps on them," said Stink.

"Maybe your letters were abducted by alien microbots," said Judy.

"Hardee-har-har. So funny I forgot to laugh."

* * *

Then one day it happened, all at once.

"It never rains, but it pours," Mum said.

Stink did not see any rain, but he did see a package. From the toy company. He tore open the box. Microbots! Monsters and spotted dogs and striped cats. Blue lions and pink mice and even a koala!

Stink read the card. "It says since my microbot didn't work, try these!"

"No fair!" said Judy. "You have all the luck."

"Knock on wood," said Stink. Just then there was a knock on the (wood!) door. Judy ran to open it.

"Parcel," said the delivery man. "For a Mr Stink Moody."

"Nobody lives here with that name," said Judy.

"Do too!" said Stink. He dropped his bots and ran to the door.

"Sign here," said the man.

"He can't even do joined-up writing!" said Judy.

"Can too!" said Stink, printing his name with curlicues to look like it was joined-up.

Stink shook the box. "I wonder what it is…"

"I wonder," said Judy. "Could it be about one million Kool Katz bars?"

"It says here they spelled *Katz* with a *K* on purpose because they thought it would look *Kool*. But they're sending me free stuff for my trouble."

Judy tried to open the box. "Hey, let me!" said Stink. His jaw dropped.

Tweezlers and Whizzles, Double Yum Bubblegum, Milk Dudes and Pay-checks, Grunts and 6th Avenues, Almost Joys and Peanut Butter Yucks.

"RARE!" said Judy. "I've never seen so many sweets."

"And don't forget the jar of chocolate-chip peanut butter, the mint green chocolate crossword puzzle and the Kool Katz baseball cap!"

"Triple rare!" said Judy.

"And it's F-R-E-E, free," said Stink. "Free as a bird! And all mine!"

Judy was mint green with envy. She wished she had two tons of special-

delivery, sign-here, free sweets and stuff. "Stink, you can't just keep all this stuff. It's like stealing or something."

"Or something," said Stink. "No way am I giving it back. I didn't take it."

Just then the phone rang. "Stink, it's for you," said Mum. "They asked for Mr Moody, and they don't mean Dad."

Mum passed the phone to Stink and went back into her office.

"Yes, I'm him … uh-huh … really? No lie? … how many do I want? … I can have twenty-five? … with monkeys? OK … yes, I think I would be satisfied."

"What?" asked Judy.

"It was the City Parks Department. I get a whole bunch of FREE monkey pencils and one free pass to the zoo! To go and see monkeys! And lemurs!"

"I'm telling," said Judy. "Mu–um!"

"Shh!" said Stink.

Mum came back into the front room. "It's not fair," Judy told her. "Stink gets tons of free stuff and he won't give me ANY and I wrote a letter once and all I got was a big fat nothing."

"Stink?" asked Mum. "What's this all about?"

"Nothing!" said Stink.

"It doesn't look like nothing."

"OK, OK. Mrs D. taught us how to write letters and I was just practising, you know, like homework..."

"Ha!" said Judy.

"And maybe I sent some letters to some people..."

"Companies!" said Judy. "Begging for free stuff!"

"No way!" said Stink. "I just told them some stuff that was wrong with things, and they sent me all this! And it's free, and no way is it stealing!" said Stink.

"Stink," said Mum, "no more letters. Later on we'll talk to Dad about what to do with all this stuff."

"Do we have to send it back?" asked Stink.

"We'll see," said Mum.

"Ha!" Judy whispered. "That means YES!"

Don't Let the Bedbugs Bite

After that, the post got way boring. No exciting letters, no mysterious parcels. Stink got a postcard about wearing a seat belt, a new issue of *Short Stuff* magazine and some envelope addressed in super-messy writing. He didn't bother opening it. Bor-ing!

Then, after dinner, as if Mum had read his mind, she told Stink out of the blue, "I almost forgot. A box came for you. It's on the table."

"Not *another* one," said Judy, hitting her forehead. "No fair. Stink, you're not supposed to write any more letters."

"I didn't!" said Stink. "I swear!"

"Don't worry. It's from someone you know and love this time," said Mum.

"Jawbreaker Heaven? Gobstoppers? I know and love them."

"No. Grandma Lou. She heard about Pyjama Day."

"Pyjama Day?" asked Judy.

"It's only in Mrs D.'s class," said Stink.

"We get to bring stuffed animals and a sleeping bag and wear pyjamas and stuff. Then we read books all day and we don't have maths and she brings her dog."

"What does her dog have to do with Pyjama Day?" asked Judy.

"I'm just saying," said Stink.

"How come Stink gets a present and not me?" asked Judy.

"It's not a present," said Stink. "It's for Pyjama Day. That's like homework."

"Just my luck," said Judy. "I have maths and spelling, and Stink gets pyjama homework." She peered over Stink's shoulder as he opened the box.

"Stop crowding," said Stink. "I need my personal space."

Judy reached into the box and snatched something. "Look! I got a Bonjour Bunny T-shirt!"

"How come you get that?" asked Stink.

"For Un-pyjama Day!" said Judy.

Stink pulled out a pair of striped PJs with bacon and eggs all over them. "No way am I wearing these for Pyjama Day," said Stink.

"Why not?" asked Mum.

"Hello! Kindergarten!" said Stink.

"Well, I think they're as cute as a bug's ear," said Mum.

Mouse raced over and licked the pyjama eggs.

"Mouse likes them!" said Judy. "Look, Stink. The sunny-side-up eggs have glow-in-the-dark middles! You love stuff that glows."

"Wait. Let me see," said Stink.

"Just try them on, honey," said Mum.

Stink pulled off his shirt and put on the pyjama top. He stretched his arms out and turned back and forth, showing off.

"Stink, you look like a walking menu. No, a night-light! No, an electric eel!" said Judy. "How will you ever get to sleep?"

"It's better than the I ♥ TRUCKS ones I got last year," said Stink. "Besides, the glow-in-the-dark part is kool-with-a-*k*!"

All of a sudden, Stink started to squirm. He scratched his arm. He scratched his neck. He pulled at the tag in the back.

"What's wrong?" asked Judy. "Your new PJs have fleas?"

"These pyjamas itch," said Stink.

"Here, I'll cut off the tags and soften

them up in the wash for tomorrow," said Mum. "You get ready for bed now, Stink. You too, Judy."

"Good night! Don't let the bedbugs bite!" Dad called from the kitchen.

"But can't I stay up until my new PJs are done?" asked Stink.

"You mean until your homework's done?" Judy laughed. "Stink loves homework so much he wants to wear it!"

IDIOM COMICS presents AS CUTE AS A BUG'S EAR by Stink J. Moody

COOL! A MAGNIFYING GLASS!

OH! LOOK AT THE TEENY TINY BUGS!

STINK SAW A BUG UP CLOSE.

WOW! I CAN EVEN SEE YOUR CUTE LITTLE EARS!

THANKS, STINK. MOST PEOPLE THINK I'M UGLY.

DON'T PUSH YOUR LUCK— I SAID YOUR EARS ARE CUTE!

Mad As a
Hornet

The next morning, Stink woke up on the sunny-side-up side of bed. He did not even count his jawbreakers or play with his microbots. Today was the day he got to wear glow-in-the-dark pyjamas to school! Double kool-with-a-*k*!

He ran downstairs. He looked under Mouse. He looked in the laundry-pile jumble on the couch. He looked on top of the washing machine. Where were his glow-in-the-dark pyjamas?

That's when he saw it.

A great big ball of lint. Not just any old mousy grey lint. A super-galactic, neon-bright, glow-in-the-dark ball of not-grey lint.

UH-OH! If this was what he thought it was, Stink was going to be as mad as a hornet! He ran to find Mum.

"Stink, honey," she told him, "I'm sorry to tell you that there was a problem with the new pyjamas."

Problem pyjamas? Pyjamas should not have problems. Maths tests should have problems. Brainteasers should have problems. Inventors should have problems.

"This?" Stink held out the super-galactic planet-sized lint ball.

"I'm afraid so," said Mum. "One wash and all the glow stuff rubbed off."

Just then, Judy rushed into the room. "Look at me! My brand-new Bonjour Bunny T-shirt. It turned alien green. I look like a lime lollipop!"

"You mean my glow-in-the-dark stuff rubbed off on her?"

"Huh?" asked Judy.

Mum held up the pyjamas. The bacon was just black wavy lines. And the sunny-side-up eggs were sunny-side-down brown mud pies.

"No way can I wear those!" said Stink.

"Think of it as scrambled eggs, Stink," said Judy.

"I could try sending them back to Grandma Lou," said Mum. "Maybe she can take them back. But you won't have any new pyjamas to wear today. Your choice."

Pyjama Day was going to be a big fat flop. Instead of way-cool glow-in-the-dark PJs, all Stink had to wear was a lousy lint ball.

"Send them back," said Stink. "Those bacon and eggs are toast."

Mum still made him write a thank-you letter to Grandma Lou, to send back with the pyjamas.

Dear Grandma Lou,

Thank you but no thank you for the pyjamas. At first I thought they were for babies, and Judy said I looked like a walking menu. Then I saw they glowed in the dark and I changed my mind, but all the glow stuff rubbed off and now I look like scrambled eggs. So I M sending them back 2 U.

I hope they didn't cost an arm and a leg and you can take them back. If not, maybe give them to the Museum of Not-Glow-in-the-Dark Pyjamas.

Maybe next time you could send me something besides homework pyjamas? (Not jawbreakers though.)

Love, Stink

While Stink was writing his letter, Judy took the pyjamas upstairs. She was up there all through breakfast. When she came back down, she announced, "Stink, I solved your pyjama problem!"

"Huh?" asked Stink.

Judy dragged Stink by the arm into the coat cupboard and shut the door. Hey! Something glowed! Like a night-light! Like a thousand and one fireflies!

"My pyjamas!" said Stink. "What did you...? How did you...?"

"I painted them with glow-in-the-dark paint!" said Judy. "So you don't have to send them back. The eggs are jellyfish now, and the bacon rashers are electric eels!"

"Jumping jawbreakers!" said Stink. "Thanks!" He hugged his sister. "This is the way-coolest ever! Now I won't be the only kid in the whole class without cool pyjamas. And I'll be the only one who glows!"

"Does this mean I can have a free chocolate bar now?" asked Judy.

"We'll see," said Stink.

IDIOM COMICS presents **That Costs an Arm and a Leg** by Stink J. Moody

THE NEW ART SHOP IS OPEN!

THE D*T SP*T ARTS & CRAFTS

STINK FOUND JUST WHAT HE WANTED.

WOW!

THE ROBO·PEN 3000! IT REMEMBERS WHAT YOU DRAW AND CAN DRAW ALL BY ITSELF!

COOL Doodle!

ROBO·PEN 3000

I SAY NICE THINGS ABOUT YOUR ART!

STINK LOOKED AT THE PRICE...

I'VE ONLY GOT TWENTY DOLLARS, BUT I'LL GIVE MY RIGHT ARM TOO!

THROW IN YOUR LEFT LEG AND YOU'VE GOT A DEAL.

MAN, THAT'S ONE PRICEY PEN!!

Double Trouble

When Stink got to class, his teacher was wearing a fuzzy THINK PINK dressing gown! She also had bunny slippers and a pillow and a real-live dog with bad breath, named Pickles.

Stink forgot all about sunny-side-down eggs. He forgot about giant lint balls. What in the world could be better than wearing not-itchy, glow-in-the-dark pyjamas to school and reading all day!

Stink plopped his sleeping bag next to his super-best-friend, Webster. "Are those your pyjamas?" he asked.

"They're not my football strip," said Webster. "But how would you know? I got them for my birthday."

Webster sure was being a grump. Stink did not know why. He hunkered down inside his sleeping bag and stuck his nose in a pop-up book of animal skeletons. He propped his head up on Fang, his two-metre-long, stuffed-animal snake. He popped a FREE fireball into his mouth.

"Want one?" he asked Webster.

"You're not allowed to eat sweets in school," said Webster. He turned the other way and stuck his nose in a book.

"Stink? Webster? Did you hear?" asked Sophie of the Elves. "We're having a Pyjama Parade. We get to walk through the corridors. And we get to go to a special assembly in the library, where Mrs Mack will tell stories from around the world. And she wears hats and plays drums. And I get to sit by you guys."

"Who cares?" said Webster.

"What's wrong with him?" Stink asked Sophie. Sophie just shrugged.

WOW! PYJAMA PARADE! ASSEMBLY! Assemblies in the library were the best! Stink could not wait to hear stories from around the world (with hats and drums).

Mrs D.'s second grade class paraded past the office and even down the fifth grade hall. In the library, Stink sat beside Sophie of the Elves. Webster was right behind Stink. Mrs D. pointed for Webster to sit down in the space right next to Stink.

"I'm not sitting by him," said Webster.

"Let's not make a mountain out of a molehill," said Mrs D.

Webster sat down.

Mrs Mack, the librarian, held up two fingers. "Let's show what good listeners we are at Virginia Dare School," she said.

"And remember," said Mrs D., "let's keep our hands to ourselves."

Stink couldn't stand being ignored. Especially by his best friend. As soon as Mrs Mack started to tell a story, Stink tapped Webster on the shoulder when he wasn't looking, just for fun.

"Hey!" said Webster. Stink pretended to be listening to the story. Webster tapped Stink on the shoulder, then pretended his hands were in his lap. Stink tapped him back. Webster tapped him back harder. "Ow!" said Stink.

"Stink!" whispered Mrs D. She pointed

to Stink and Webster to settle down and keep quiet.

"You guys are in trouble!" whispered Sophie of the Elves.

"Now," said Mrs Mack, "we're going to turn down the lights and travel to deepest Africa. I hope you like scary stories!"

The lights went out. Stink glowed like a night-light! Mrs D. was sure to see him if he tapped Webster now. Stink pulled both of his arms all the way inside his pyjama shirt, just to be safe. He did not want his tapping fingers to get him into any more trouble.

Drumbeats filled the air. Mrs Mack made her voice low and whispery. The folktale was all about the Bad One, this spooky voice coming from inside a cave. The voice sounded so big and bad it was scaring all the other animals in the rainforest. At the end, the Bad One turned out to be nothing but a centipede. Phew! A South African red-legged centipede!

Stink knew all about centipedes. "Once, in the Toad Pee Club with my sister," he told Webster, "we tried to set a record for the longest human centipede."

"So?" said Webster.

Stink forgot all about paying attention. Something was wrong with Webster. He tried to make up a centipede joke to tell Webster.

"What goes ninety-nine clunk?" Stink asked Webster. "Or thirty-three clunk? Or sixty-seven clunk?" Webster ignored him. "A centipede with a broken leg!" Stink cracked up. He flashed his fireball-red tongue at Webster. Webster did not even crack a smile.

Mrs Mack was asking, "How many legs does a centipede have?" Stink knew the answer. He went to raise his hand, but his arms were still inside his pyjama shirt.

"One hundred!" said someone in the front row.

Stink knew one hundred was not the whole answer. He just had to raise his hand. He tried to raise an elbow from inside his shirt.

Something was wrong. Very wrong. Something had happened to Stink's pyjama top. It had shrink-shrank-shrunk! Stink wiggled and wriggled and tried to worm his way out of the

shirt. Help! Where were the armholes?
It was still dark. He couldn't see a thing.
His shirt was all twisted. His arms were
all caught. His elbows poked inside his
shirt like a punch-bag, but he couldn't
find his way out.

Help! Stink was stuck inside his
pyjama top!

"The name *centipede* means 'one
hundred feet'. That's why we think all
centipedes have a hundred legs," said
Mrs Mack.

Stink was still wrestling with his
pyjamas. The top went up over his

head. Stink lost his head! He wrestled some more. Finally! He poked his arm out!

"Ow!" he heard Webster cry. "Hey, you sucker-punched me!" He shoved Stink into Sophie of the Elves.

"Hey!" said Stink. "I was only —"

"Boys!" said Mrs D. "Come with me."

First the shirt. Then hitting Webster. Double trouble!

All the lights were on now. The room was suddenly somebody-got-in-trouble quiet. Webster had his head down and looked like he was going to cry. Everybody stared at the boys as they followed Mrs Dempster out into the corridor.

"OK, you two. What's this fighting all about? I thought you were the best of friends."

"Stink started it," said Webster. "I

was just sitting there, and he punched me for no reason."

"I didn't mean to hit him! Honest!" said Stink. "It's all my pyjamas' fault. I got stuck inside my shirt! Cross my heart. No lie. I was just trying to raise my hand to say that most centipedes have fifteen pairs of legs. But some have up to 177 pairs, and if a leg gets cut off, it grows back, and some centipedes even glow in the dark."

"So it was an accident?" asked Mrs Dempster.

"Yes!" said Stink.

"Can you say you're sorry, Stink?"

"Sorry, Webster," said Stink. "I didn't mean to hit you."

"Webster?" said Mrs Dempster. "Are you OK now? Do you need to go and see the nurse?"

"Whatever," said Webster.

"Boy," Stink said. "I never knew pyjamas could get a person into so much trouble!" But Webster was already walking down the corridor towards the nurse's office. His back was mad. Even his hair was mad.

Feel Like a Heel

Stink felt lousy. Worse than a NOT-one-hundred-legged centipede. He dragged himself home from school, down the street, along the pavement, and in through the front door.

Dad was home early. "How was Pyjama Day?" he asked Stink.

"Terrible," said Stink. "I had one of those terrible, horrible, no good, very bad, just-like-that-kids'-book yuck days."

"What's wrong?" asked Mum, coming into the room.

"Stink hit his friend Webster today!" said Judy. "At the library assembly. It was all over school. He got in way-big trouble and the teacher took him out and yelled at him up and down and the whole school saw and —"

"That's enough, Judy," said Dad.

"It wasn't my fault," said Stink. "It was my pyjamas' fault!" Stink told Mum and Dad what happened. "I'm going to write a letter to the pyjama people and tell them their pyjamas got me in big trouble *and* made me lose my best friend," said Stink.

"No more letters!" said Judy.

"No more letters," said Mum.

"Well, maybe one more," said Dad. "How about a letter of apology to your friend Webster?"

✷ ✷ ✷

Stink went upstairs. He hid the troublemaker PJs in the way-back of his bottom drawer, where the pinchy underwear, socks with holes, and the too-baby I ♥ TRUCKS pyjamas from last year were.

Then Stink worked on the letter as if it was homework.

Dear Webster,
I am really really really really really really really really sorry I punched you when I was just trying to tell about centipedes. Don't be mad at me any more. Please please please with jawbreakers on top.
Sincerely,
Super-Sorry Stink

Stink searched around his desk for an envelope. He would put the letter on Webster's desk tomorrow. Hello! What was this? Under a pile of jawbreakers, Stink found an envelope. Not an empty envelope. A messy-handwriting envelope addressed to Stink Moody. As in him!

All of a sudden Stink remembered getting the messy-writing letter. But he'd been too busy counting his jawbreakers to even open it! He ripped it open now.

YOU ARE INVITED said the card. It was spelled out in balloons held by gorillas. The card was from Webster. It was for his birthday party. And his birthday party was Saturday. LAST Saturday.

Stink had missed Webster's birthday!

Now he knew why Webster was such a grump. Stink felt like a heel. No, he felt like 177 pairs of heels. Worse than a broken-legged centipede. Stink felt like a stinkbug.

He had to think of some way to make it up to Webster. They just had to be friends again. Had to!

Stink thought and thought. He petted Mouse. He petted Toady. He scratched his head a lot. Scratching your head was supposed to help you think, right? All it did was make him look like he had fleas.

At last, Stink had an idea. He went downstairs to get Dad in on his idea. Then he finished the letter to Webster.

P.S. I missed your party because I never got the invitation. I mean I got it but it was hiding under a LOT of jawbreakers. I guess I was so into my jawbreakers, I forgot everything else. You will get a special birthday surprise. Better than a letter. All I can say is LOOK OUT!

Hint: It starts with the letters CG (but you'll never ever guess!).

IDIOM COMICS presents

I Feel Like a Heel

by Stink J. Moody

A Leopard CAN Change Its Spots

Stink got to school early and slipped the letter inside Webster's desk. He watched Webster read it. Webster looked up. He looked over at Stink. "You mean you didn't miss my birthday on purpose?"

"No way," said Stink. "Just like I didn't sucker-punch you on purpose. You gotta believe me."

Webster grinned from ear to ear.

"Friends?" asked Stink.

"Friends," said Webster. "So what's

the big surprise, huh? What's CG? C'mon! Tell me! I can't wait!"

"My lips are sealed," said Stink, zipping his lips.

"Does it stand for *Card Game*?" asked Webster.

"*Cinderella's Glass slipper*?" asked Sophie of the Elves.

"*Cucumbers and Grapes?*" asked Webster. "*Crazy Glue?*"

"No, no and nope," said Stink. "You just have to wait. My dad's bringing it. But Mrs D. said not until the end of the day."

✷ ✷ ✷

Waiting was harder than writing letters. Harder than punctuation. Harder than spelling *sincerely*.

At the end of the day, Mrs D. read eleven pages from Sophie of the Elves' favourite chapter book about a brave mouse and an evil rat.

Finally! At last! An announcement over the PA system.

"Special delivery for Class 2D! Stink Moody to the front office!"

"Wow! Cool! Hey! What? Huh?" everybody buzzed.

Stink walked-not-ran down to the office and came back to class with Dad, a rainbow-bright rooster piñata and 21,280 jawbreakers. Not to mention all sorts of chocolate bars, microbots and monkey pencils.

"Candy-Gram!" Stink announced. "I repeat. Candy-Gram for Webster Gomez."

Webster was already at the door. He had never ever seen so many sweets in his whole entire life. "For me? WOWEE!"

"To celebrate your birthday," said Stink. "With the whole class!"

"Piñata party!" everybody was saying.

"A Candy-Gram!" said Sophie of the Elves. "*CG* is for *Candy-Gram*!"

"I never got a Candy-Gram before. It's like a telegram, only better."

"Where'd you get all the sweets and stuff?" asked Sophie.

"I got them FREE. Sort of by mistake on purpose."

Dad and Mrs D. filled the piñata

with sweets and goodies. Dad got to stand on the teacher's desk! He hung the piñata from the ceiling.

"Who wants to go first?" asked Dad, holding out the blindfold.

"Webster!" called Stink.

Dad put the blindfold on Webster and handed him the stick. "Stand back, everybody," Dad called.

"On the count of three!" said Mrs D.

Webster swung the stick. It sliced the air, this way and that. *Whoosh! Swoosh!*

"Go, Webster, go!" everybody yelled. "Over this way. You're getting warm!"

Bam! Webster finally hit the piñata! Nothing. Class 2D was super-quiet.

"Let's try again – in French," said Mrs D. *"Un, deux, trois…"* Bam! Webster hit the piñata again! Still nothing.

"That rooster doesn't want to crow," said Dad.

"I'll help!" called Stink. "Let's swing the stick together."

"Third time lucky," said Mrs D. "Give it your best try. In Spanish, everybody! *Uno, dos, tres…"*

Ka-POW! Webster and Stink hit the piñata again. *Bam! Bam! Bam! Crack!* They cracked open the piñata.

Cock-a-doodle-doo! The rooster let out a loud sound, for real! Everybody screamed. A flood of sweets rained down. Jawbreakers and Tweezlers, Milk Dudes and Peanut Butter Yucks. The kids raced to the front. They grabbed sweets from all over the floor, under desks, behind the bookcase, even in the bin.

"It's raining cats and dogs!" said Stink. "Kool Katz and Scottie dogs!"

"We really hit the jackpot!" said Webster.

"That was more fun than a barrel of monkeys!" said Sophie of the Elves.

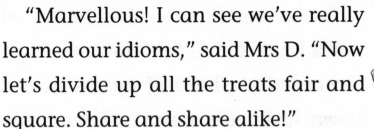

"Marvellous! I can see we've really learned our idioms," said Mrs D. "Now let's divide up all the treats fair and square. Share and share alike!"

Stink stared at his own sweet pile of treats and treasures on his desk. It was  a lot smaller than 21,280 jawbreakers. But when he saw Webster's face, and a whole classful of grins, he felt good inside. UN-rotten to the core, like the sweet, gooey bubblegum centre of a jawbreaker.

"I'm proud of you, Stink," said Dad. "I think you proved a leopard CAN change its spots."

"I like the way you and your dad worked together," said Mrs D., smiling. "Two heads *are* better than one."

"And friends are better than all the free stuff in the world," said Stink.

"Is that another idiom?" asked Webster.

"No, it's a Stink-iom!" said Stink.

LIST OF IDIOMS
(in order of appearance)

- kid in a candy shop
- get out of the wrong side of bed
- rotten to the core
- sour grapes
- strike a deal
- finger-lickin' good
- down in the dumps
- A leopard can't change its spots.
- Two heads are better than one
- You can't teach an old dog new tricks.
- Practice makes perfect.
- It never rains, but it pours.
- Put your thinking cap on.
- knock on wood
- His jaw dropped.
- free as a bird
- green with envy
- Don't let the bedbugs bite.
- out of the blue
- just my luck
- as cute as a bug's ear
- mad as a hornet
- cost an arm and a leg
- double trouble
- make a mountain out of a molehill
- lost his head
- cross my heart
- feel like a heel
- grin from ear to ear
- My lips are sealed.
- You're getting warm.
- third time lucky
- It's raining cats and dogs.
- hit the jackpot
- more fun than a barrel of monkeys
- fair and square
- share and share alike

Be sure to check out Stink's adventures!

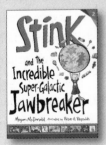

In the mood for Stink's older sister Judy Moody? Then try these!

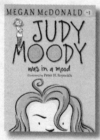

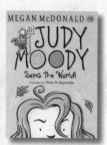

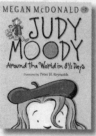

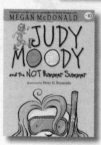

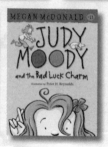

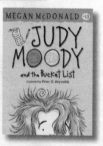